Breaking Out To Freedom
Red
Marina Dobrosavljevic
M

Sometimes the hurt is so immense. Forgiving is possible but the hurt remains changing our being forever, possibly we no longer have strength to ever return to our original selves , longing forever for our innocence and wholeness yet it remains a distant memory.

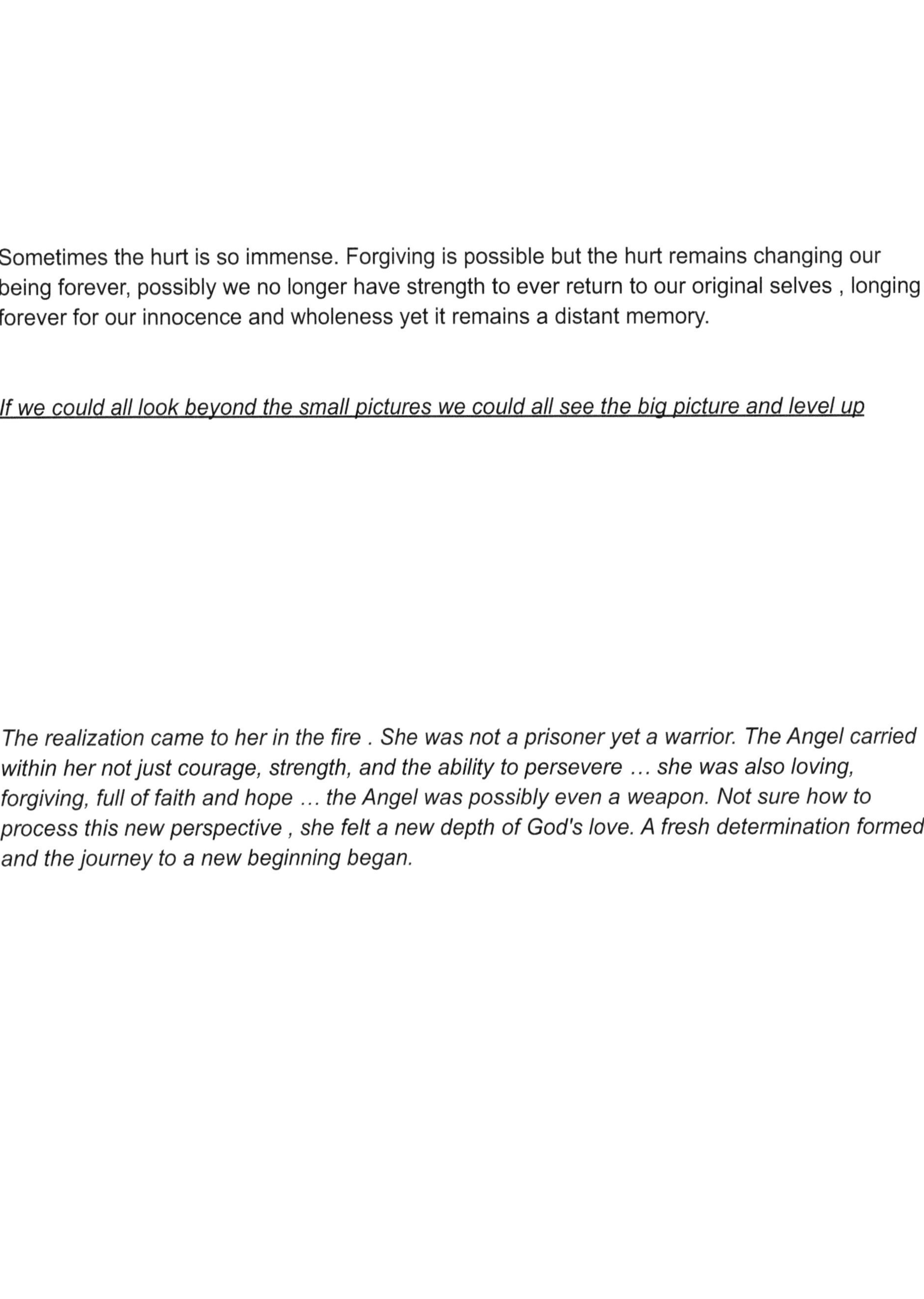

The realization came to her in the fire . She was not a prisoner yet a warrior. The Angel carried within her not just courage, strength, and the ability to persevere … she was also loving, forgiving, full of faith and hope … the Angel was possibly even a weapon. Not sure how to process this new perspective , she felt a new depth of God's love. A fresh determination formed and the journey to a new beginning began.

As I would do anything for my child… For him I have an understanding and a patience , I am determined to not fail as a parent ….I imagine God feels about me. I at times felt differently , as if I was misunderstood by the Lord, as if I was so appalling but over time I realized this way that I am as a mother ….the love I naturally have , that is in the likeness of our Creator , actually an imperfect likeness ..yet if I accept that I am loved and accepted ,meaningful and important to God even if as much as I imperfectly accept and love my child than I feel peace. I realized a lot of my hurt and insecurities were perspective, and yes life has hurt ..my environment has disappointed and confused me, but I also have many blessings
…Much strength and perseverance that I can't explain , except through faith , thru the fact that I am a child of God. I always feel also that I carry a responsibility to show God the depth of my love, the willingness and desire to fight for the Lord to do my best , seems all that is expected of me is to do right by me and others , live a life that is good and kind, meaningful and of service…that's really what's best for me anyway.

……..

A FINAL TEAR FELL…A REALIZATION THAT THE EMOTIONS MUST BE SILENCED, NUMBED…THE TEARS THEY RESOLVE NOTHING, I JUST WALLOW IN THEM… DROWN- AND DEVASTATED I FALL APART … WELL NO MORE, THE TEARS I WILL DRY, THE PAIN I WILL NOT ALLOW TO RULE MY HEART.

****

So many times in my life I waited for happiness and fulfillment, yet now looking back I realized I was fulfilled and happy just not cherishing the moment. In our society we have milestones and timelines …so many expectations from others that we forget to value our own timeline and to respect our wants and what we actually are satisfied with. It's one of those damned if you do and damned if you don't and somehow we are wired to always imagine a different decision, action, way of living our lives would have been a better outcome ,always wondering what if … I do imagine we all one day realize we are just perfectly in tune with our own destiny and once we remove what we allow others to dictate for our lives we realize we are living our own moment , sailing our own sails ….hopefully we all at one point realize we are in our best place whether that be chasing a dream, growing and evolving in that particular moment , or simply enjoying ourselves without comparison to others ways or accomplishments. I do think it's nice to find inspiration from others whether it be to figure out our own way or to get motivated in our own direction but I also think when we seek this path we sadly pay attention to the wrong details and we then have the opposite effect in our feelings and decisions. Let's rewire our perspective and perceptions.

*****

MY WAY

I put my foot down
In this moment I say
Your route is great for you
But I will go live my way

I do not require the same things
I value that which brings me joy
I feel my own emotions
My life I cannot play with as a toy

Going down a path which is already trodden
It makes me feel empty and fake
Although my ways are unique and misunderstood
I my life by the reins take

The only judge I look to is above
I must to myself be true
And I may not meet society's standards
But I just gotta my way things do

In life I have learned
My respect I need to exist
I am the one I answer to
And to listen I persist

******

There a conflict arose…her heart seemed to be split into pieces , she was confused whether this battle was internal or if her fate was on the line. Has this game evolved to a point where she could not follow along. Confused ,hurt, yet still faith gave her the strength. Realizing thru the ordeal that she had much to learn about herself. Before her destiny could unfold she had to learn and possibly even make a decision for her life which could change her destiny. So unsure of the decisions for her life she looked to God …no longer did she want to fall to unknowing or not realizing facts around her. She however was sure about one thing -whatever the future held she would chase her dreams, she would contribute, and no -she would not numb her emotions, she faced all of them head on realizing she even misunderstood so much and brought on unnecessary pain in times past….this all gave her hope that in the future she would feel more realistically. Also -she realized she was unique…parts of her were only to her understandable

,she felt God was the one who really understood her most, she had gained strength through her ordeal figuring this split heart could possibly form a whole ,imagining God would heal the scars and use the love that was given and received and create something beautiful….she knew she would be ok.

****

I wonder at times would God allow me to show others a better way, in my heart I feel this is my calling … yet- is it even wanted ? Would it make a difference?…. Could my words and my actions make such a difference to where a different life is possible ? I wondered always about my purpose ,much of my passion comes from love , it's natural yet I do question if it is my life's challenge to make this change , a purpose of mine to show and share with others …to bring unity and awaken mankind….or is my challenge to accept that although this is my nature it is not possible to do much in this life …is my challenge to accept that which does not make sense to me and find understanding to why this must be the way. I have faith however that although I am unsure of my place , future, or the secrets of creation… I will fulfill my destiny just as it is to be fulfilled.
*****

CREATION

With the years magic has multiplied
Baffled at the marvel which is life
I have no explanations for many occurrence
Yet I believe it is my fight

I must accept my own truth
I must battle societies ways
My mission in life is to find confidence
To accept the purpose for my days

As I learn about myself
I seem to also learn about those in my world
I have my own vision
Too far I was never lured

I doubt my own existence
Yet the universe throws proof my way
I observe and soak up information
Sometimes I do not know what to think or say

It's hard to even accept the proof
I fight to not doubt too much
I think many live in illusion
And I to dreams clutch

I believe my purpose is as big as any
Yet I also think it to be small
I am here to fulfill God's plan
He lifts me every time I begin to fall

I see the value of those I encounter
I believe life's lessons lead me down the path
I live in love and hope
I pray for mercy from God's wrath

I think my imperfections
They allow me to forgive
My insecurities are many
Yet my confidence builds the longer I live.

****

She remained confused, remembering the words of the crowd…" you have to help us, you will lead us amongst the planets to eternity towards God. You need to teach us and then you will have love. " The Angel wept remembering the bird, she loved him so much. They told her there were many birds once we headed on our journey. The Angel did not understand, it made no sense to her that any other love was even possible yet somehow a part of her realized that her happiness depending on the fact that she had the freedom to follow her heart, to decide and to make her own decision on who she would share her life with, of course God would be the one to guide her to make her final decision , she after all knew not their hearts. The Angel wondered why she was lied to that only one option laid before her so long ago, did the dishonesty come from love or trickery? Firmly she decided she would dismiss the need to know, infact she would rather believe the best in others….it had to be from love. In the end of it God to her was always in control ,she assumed regardless of all against or for her nothing was as relevant as God and her destiny. She carefully decided to make her choice carefully …her future in love would need to be less turbulent than her past.

****

Sometimes we misunderstand others' way of showing us their love. We assume our love language, actions, and demeanor are all the same but it's twisted when the person you love has the opposite way of showing love ….when you cannot feel confident that they feel for you since they are not expressing it in a way you understand…. Yet they are the one whose love you want, you end up confused and for some reason it works that they do not get what it is you require as a validation or they are unable to express in the way you need love to be shown to you , it leaves this empty feeling…this misunderstanding between lovers which cannot find a common ground .

****

I wonder at times about life
The mysterious journey on which we all embark
Nobody is quite sure of anything
We just go towards the finish looking back to start

We search for happiness
We long for love
We find strength when it's hard
Many their courage get from above

I wonder does each occurrence have a purpose
Is it all without much reason
We don't know yet we proceed
As nature we go from season to season

We form …we evolve
We over time change
Realizing wisdom and patience
They come with experience…with age

Over time the little things nag at us
Hopefully we all realize what we really hold dear
Live our life according to our own standard
Realize failing sometimes is not a thing to fear

With lost opportunities
We still find the courage to try
It's important to participate in life
Not be a bystander watching it pass by

****

LOVE

I longed my whole life for love
I searched all over it to find
I believed it would be given as a gift
I shut my eyes and looked -blind

I at times imagined I could grow it
I quickly realized it does not work in that way
I also tried to force it
Lost hope with each passing day

Somehow for me love seems out of reach
It's possible I never learned how to feel
I approached this emotion wrong
And now pain is my main deal

I no longer believe this love thing is even big
Who cares if all this time I was able to survive
Love was lacking yet I continued
I can even say I have joy …I thrive

Looking back I realize in my search
Instead of love I always found hurt
I was abused, disrespected, and belittled
Love treated me as unimportant….kicked me as dirt

Now I no longer even want to feel loved
I don't like the way I felt in the past
I no longer believe or hope in a companion
I now know people for me don't last

Partly I think I may be the problem
My expectations may be high
But I refuse to add to the hurt myself
I can just love myself till the day I die

My wants in love may be too big
I want equality and care
I want to feel understood and connected
I also don't want to share

I can't find the one for all this time
This love thing is such a struggle for me
As time goes by in life
I slowly die the passion and no longer a way do I see

******

"TEAM LOSS"

The world turns
Tragic events unfold
We wither away
Drift from young to old

Our hearts break to tragedies
We live trying to stop the chaos
Our hurdles we tackle
The attacks continue to get us

We see that things are bad
Yet we can't pinpoint the cause
We hope bandaid solutions will work
Yet the evils show us they're boss

Our hearts accustomed to breaking
Our value is taken away
We pray…we hope …we keep going
More sadness in the new day

We forget the value of life
Slowly we are freezing inside
We smile we push forward
While our pain we push down and hide

We rely on someone to figure it out
Yet the whole time the answer is within us all
We need to hold and uplift one another
Otherwise collectively we fall

****

Sometimes I feel very hurt by the world in general, my environment, the people around me, the leaders ….all of it. I feel hurt for me, I feel hurt for everyone it's like as a society we are just full blown disrespectful in every essence of the word… and I think about God, I feel hurt on behalf of Him . We look to the Heavens and we wait for salvation while we throw dirt in the same direction. With closed eyes and shut up hearts, with minds on autopilot we belittle ourselves, we symbolically show God that no we do not want what God offers , we ask for it yet in our lives we gravitate and tightly grasp the complete opposite.
****

****

Neptune, Jupiter, Pluto…. The Universe beyond, I a citizen of Earth that wonders what existence surrounds. I wonder if anyone on Earth has more answers than I, when do we learn of the mysteries … are we a spec , stardust, souls , or all of it and more in one. I question my place, I wonder about parts of me…I sometimes even think there's more than what I hear and what I see. A child of God, a piece in Creation, yet how do I fill my role if I'm constantly rerouted , placed in the dark, manipulated , lied to …. I want to trust my instincts but my perception is tainted from life, in the end I know God is the only one who can guide me, direct me, and mold us all accordingly, with the love of a Father for a daughter or son . I don't demand to know all secrets , I don't think I could handle as much… but in this life and in this world I am lost without God ,my safety without the Lord is questionable , that is all which I blindly trust. I know I am not perfect, I attempt always to correct my ways , yet it seems growth is constant , I form as I live out my days. We all learn lessons , evolve in our own ways…. I wonder if in my lifetime I will see the outcome of Creation coming together, each of us with our unique contribution… will I be a part of the end and the beginning in some way.

****

And her heart could only revive through God's love. She feared nothing knowing that God held her very being , after all He is her safe place, her protector, teacher and guide through it all. Her courage grew as she grew confident in her faith . The comfort that was with the Lord it eased her pain and fears, she felt less alone once these realizations formed. She knew she would forever be understood, she found a place where her truth was not too much, her emotions were safe here …and slowly life began.

****

When I think about the future I worry, I always have , somehow I have this nagging feeling that this destruction and that the evil ways of so many have to stop . I fear what kind of world is coming and I watch so many fall to manipulations and those that don't are very few. We allow our egos and our prejudice, the poisons we were given …they smear our actions and taint our perceptions . Somehow I think we are all aware yet so much hurt and lack of healing has brought us to the point where we can't hold ourselves to a standard where we act on our true good nature. Sadly we live with the effects and continue to bow down because that is the norm. Constantly our conscience and our humanity ,our very core are ignored and pushed down because we have it instilled in us that standing out …thinking and doing different….it just seems ludacris- we fear being rejected or mocked so we follow the crowd…. This is what we are from a young age trained to feel …it's embedded so deep and it is a weakness which is used against us all.
****

And the Angel realized that she too had been tricked yet God never forgot her she was overjoyed that she was cared about . After all the biggest love that ever existed was from and for God, without it no other love would be possible, God is love! Although she knew her imperfections were many a new determination formed with the knowledge that God would guide her. She felt that all those times that she feared her heart's desire to forgive and love , to aid and comfort ….they were not actually anything negative , God was not so to be angry at the depth of her heart…she realized God had created those depths within her ..God had molded and guided, and taught her …been there the whole time …that which she loved most yet others shunned about her …those things were beautifully crafted by God. She was overjoyed that although she had errored in her life , there were parts which God did not allow to rot away or be tossed out- those were the parts she valued and loved most about herself. Forever grateful to the Lord for His mercy and protection. These parts of her helped her recover from her fall…these parts were her strength, these parts made her find a way to forgive and even love herself too.
****

I came to a point in my life where I had to reevaluate what my priorities truly were. I was missing the fullness of my emotions, goals, values. It was a hard process and I'm still living it , I think I will revisit and reconstruct as needed but in this process I found myself. I realized so much about myself such as what I will and will not tolerate for my life. I feel that if I don't respect my boundaries and expectations that I will always be unsatisfied. I also realized that a big problem I have is that I love deeply and have a hard time accepting the bad in those I love allowing hurt that they bring me to be prolonged… and I don't mean that offensively -nobody's perfect I guess-I'm sure parts of my behavior actions and way of life don't sit right with others too ,I think that's normal but I can't find a way to settle I think life has so much to offer and that I am not obligated to lower my standard or expectations, I don't expect anyone to do it either….I actually think a big problem in the world is that we suck it up , why? Sure there are circumstances where that is the only reasonable option but we let it trickle over to things we shouldn't settle on . But for me it's so overwhelming when I have to deal with stuff I'm fully aware I don't have to take or accept ,it really affects my mood and my peace …. I feel it's very unhealthy ,not sure if that's how others feel , if maybe it's something I'm hyper sensitive to possibly but in the end of it my best for myself and those around me is to respect myself my wants my needs and my terms.

****

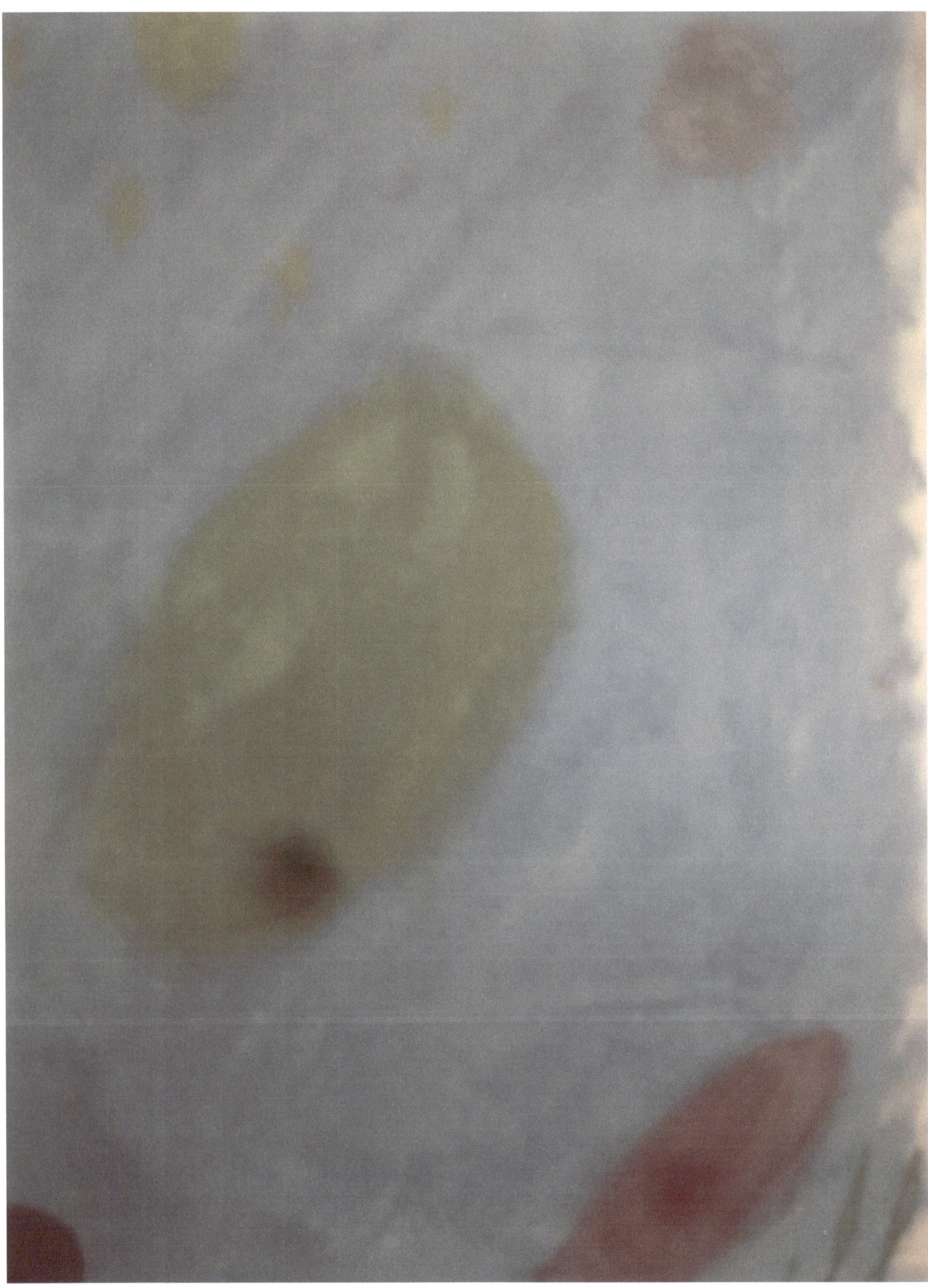

Wonder

So much wonder fills me
I find it in my present my future even my past
Life is so magical
In motion from first day to last
The connections within us all
I wonder how far they go
From history to future
Yet the present is all we really know
Sometimes it is scary to imagine
The possibilities are so many
The questions are all we can be sure of
Lucky if we get answers to any
Is it wrong to be curious?
Is it right to wander into the unknown?
How can we not know it's entire essence
Yet in our environment feel at home?
The nature which is independent of us
How do we intertwine?
The vastness of existence
What really is time?
Reality ….is it perspective?
Society… can it reform?
Spirituality and religion such mysteries
Is life after death or is it only when born?
****

Reluctant to settle…Reluctant to walk away

Fear overcomes me
I imagine the hurt he will bring
I feel as if my expressions will always be ignored
Even now my needs don't mean a thing

It's as if he picks at my wounds
He wants to see how much they will bleed
Instead of reassuring my value
On my hurt his ego seems to feed

I question what it is I am fighting for
I imagine at least alone I feel secure
Is love worth the gamble
Our pasts now our futures obscure

The unsureness of it all
It stops me in my track
Somehow walking the road alone
Aware it's love I lack

The problem really is in fact
Maybe even me
If I could find confidence in our love
I can't imagine what the problem would be

It is somehow discouraging tho
You seem to get angry at my confusion
You allow the hurt to simmer
Maybe you don't care after all is my conclusion.

****

"Yet Again"

Again over and over
You trickle into my mind
I dismiss your very appearance
You are in a past time

I tell my ego to calm down
Yet aware the problem I want to avoid
I somehow had my hopes up
You seemed to be the cure for my heart's void

I admit I want to stop this all
I just don't want to feel for you
Yet it's irrelevant how you feel
Doesn't matter what you do

I can't say you're an only love
I can't say I won't go on
I just know you have a place in my heart
And it's not a feeling I can out run

I don't have petty hurtful wishes
I actually hope for you the best
I do however feel I am out of space
My heart too full yet tired and needing rest

I wonder do I reside in someone's being
Does someone carry a torch for me
Or am I just someone to break
When will this torment just let me be

I can't say I even have strength
This broken heart it's had enough
Somehow I wish I could just be satisfied
Alone yet happy although it's rough

I tell myself I am built to be this way
Someone who is misunderstood and alone
But I am human and I feel
I do wish for a companion to call home.

****

"Your Love"

In the depth of my soul
I carry you around
I walked away thinking it will pass
But just heartbreak I found

I think back and regret so much
I can't go back and change a thing
And you don't care about my emotions
Days you to me do not bring

Strange how it doesn't matter
Anything that you don't do
My feelings are enormous
I'm stuck on you like glue

Even with my broken heart
I manage you to love
And as the days go on I do question
Are you my punishment or blessing from above

I imagined that a love this huge
It would take the care of two
Yet I learn as time goes on
It just takes the existence of you

I remember many things I ran from
I carry so much of the blame
You gave up on us
And I was never again the same

You spoke to me with looks
Your eyes held the galaxy that was mine
It's as if you are physically gone
Yet I carried you in my heart the whole time

I question how fair it is
Is it nice another man to pursue
Will I ever be able to put out this flame I carry
Or will I forever be blue
****

Her armor was her defense as it all paused. Realizing she would need to face the internal battle she had. Inside of her battled light and dark, she struggled to find first a balance but soon realized that balance was not the problem, the problem was to survive while striving for something new ….this improved version of her and her life it could only come with this soul search, she had to be completely open with herself …she found comfort that God would help heal parts of her which she found appalling. She came to one huge problem though , this same problem forever haunted her LOVE. Somehow she couldn't avoid confronting herself ,all of her emotions, as well as her past .She was very aware of the fact that although there lay multiple love options none of them were actually a choice she could have, it seemed impossible so she did not approach it as a choosing ,instead deciding to accept and find closure for each of them. Actually facing this fact helped her learn what the problems have always been …. She also accepted why things had not worked out in the past. Then came the realization that she did not want to spread hurt, she felt pain deeply and could not wish these feelings on anyone else , relying on her faith to guide her through this lesson about her own existence as a woman and her ways in love , she hoped eventually she would come out the wiser and more emotionally available, but she also was sceptical wondering if maybe love for her was not destined.

The Angel patiently went on with the days, her fears were silenced by the Lord , God was her shield and her armor, her comfort and compass. Although she knew not how to make sense of even herself she knew that it didn't matter too much. Possibly her purpose in Creation was to rely on her faith in God more than others , she actually felt it was safest and made most sense that way. In this world and in this life she knew she was blind to much and that which she did know and see it was hard to make sense of . The world had infected her with it's poisons ,the cure was in her faith, and her love for the Lord.

As her contemplation progressed she realized the big issue with her feelings and actions had always been the first love ,the one which never got a chance. Her own fears of the vastness of her feelings for him , they had her run away yet she could never find happiness with another. She really even tried to downplay her emotions she deep down tried to ignore them because of some strange fear of the love not working out or that she would disappoint him, only now realizing she had only disappointed herself. Now she had to accept that he may never be hers that he was happy , she dreaded her sadness and hurt, it was made worse by the realization that she wasn't sure if it was that's she had mostly herself to blame it if the circumstances were just not ok. Forced to play with the idea that maybe it was not all her fault, it was hard to accept that she was loved and wanted so it was hard to accept that it was simply not possible because of love , possibly her emotions would not allow her to proceed forward ever because in the end it would hurt someone and she loved too much , and held herself to a higher standard….she could not do what everyone else does and shame love…twist love ..be careless and uncaring with love …to her that was labelling something as love which it was not. Regardless of her not knowing which version of closure was appropriate for the situation she gave that combination closure anyway

****

"You and I"

Us two we are one
Physically separated
But in my heart we live
This love was never done

Somehow fate separated us
Somehow insecurities took the lead
Time didn't erase the depth of my love
Memories I to my broken heart feed

I do realize however
I may need to go the rest alone
I don't know how to get you back
But I can't allow my heart to turn to stone

Maybe God has other forms of love for me
Possibly I cannot ever have you
I can't imagine it being fair to be with another
Alone I choose to hope for you

I search for you in my dreams
I think of you constantly in the day
Sometimes I feel you in my being
Carry you inside me in every way

Yet I cannot change any emotion
You cannot change your moves
I accept we are not destined
Maybe it's a win… in the end we don't really lose

Possibly it is so for a reason
I either way cannot help but to care
Nobody can change how they feel
I guess it's better you are over there

I finally thought out realistically
How much our union would hurt others we love
Although you and I have a love story
We just weren't meant by God above

I don't know how to even not love you
But I do know to move on I will succeed

I now can finally shut our door
Heal my wounds so they stop to bleed.
****

Love it is this day an age something many fear yet we can't help but crave it, we need love…many are determined to surpress their emotions because sadly the world we are in has taught us that they make us weak….yet we cannot shut them down , and we can only ignore them for so long. There comes a point in our lives where we choose whether we will be fools but human and correct the way we are created or if we will evolve into monsters and in the process hurt not just those around us but ourselves as well. When our last breath leaves will it be one of peace following a life or content or of regret from living ahalf life. On our last day do we wake up but have no choice but to accept the way we chose to live finally seeing we denied ourselves the basics of life. Love it is powerful it can create ,it can destroy…but it can never disappear in completeness.

The Angel was hurt having to face that maybe it was those she had come to love who set her up, knowing deep down it may not have been as heartless and spiteful as she believed. It was the fact that her suffering was so immense which made her feel more sensitive she thought to herself ,possibly actually being correct. The Angel refused to be bitter, she accepted that maybe the situation she was in was a part of her purpose and destiny…. She prayed those which had harmed her intentionally or unknowingly , hoping they had changed for the better that they valued their life as well as others for whom they care, she hoped her pain was not in vain and that from it came positivity and an abundance of joy for at least others if not herself, she cared very little anyway …her reward being with the Lord, the Angel looked forward to the day when she would have peace… God was her guide and ultimate focus…she looked to grow and faithfully awaited the guidance she long prayed for, she wanted to be positive in the world and positive to those around her …she was born to make it through this and not ever allow difficulty to deter her from success.
****

For some reason my nature won't allow me to dwell on someone's bad intention, I cannot just flip on the hate feeling when I'm hurt, betrayed, or disappointed. It's something I don't understand but I like about myself. I guess a part of me knows how easy it is to give in to the dark part of our human nature, I know how much work ,patience, and will it takes to tap into that which is the light inside of us. The light side of our being forgives, it is not only healthy but crucial I believe, if we constantly give in to the dark side of our beings if that is where we find comfort and joy ,if we become accustomed to ill feelings and hate -if we carry grudges and constantly seek revenge well we really are hurting ourselves. We lose the opportunity to live in a peaceful and loving way, we replace joy with misery in our being because logically hate and holding grudges that does not heal ….it simmers and grows us into monsters ,but forgiving and finding a way to heal ourselves we grow the light dwelling deep inside of us …it's like picking a different road , it really effects so much how we choose to handle things that happen to us. Our personalities and our character form as we age and these choices are a part of what we form into.

*****"

"How?"

The hurt which was intentional
I cannot return it your way
I choose to accept it happened
Heal myself now ,in this new day

I will use your actions as a tool
Your weapons they only caused growth
I will not change my nature to soothe the ego
I will forgive and do better going forth

I cannot answer if it was known
If it just didn't matter at all
But I took your kick and learned how to fly
I had to escape my fall

I think your actions only show
What it is you carry within
It helps me understand human nature
It gives me insight into sin

My heart cannot help but be in pain
Yet I know strength takes the lead

I will not wish harm your way
I inside me plant a good seed

Your nature is something to be corrected
I will not change my ways
Somehow I think I will heal
Evolve be better off from my past days

It is devastating to face the truth
The world it has so little love
But I do know one thing for sure
It's most important to be loved from above

Your evil ways in the end you face
It's you who is at a loss
Maybe you win what you value
But what's valuable you aside toss

The things that matter to me
I know are things unique
I do wonder why I'm in this struggle
I ask the Lord when we speak

I have no explanation
But in me I have a strong faith
I know I can overcome your attacks
On God's time- I'm never late

I worry about humanity
I see how selfish and uncaring we are
I see how lost we wander
Our hearts have a callus or a deep scar

We cannot make the right choices
We do not see what is right
We all just struggle and claw thru life
We scream and put up a fight

And as we see we make wrong choices
We continue to do it anyway
Our lights are dimmed
I know-so how could I angry stay.

****

I think it's important in life that we consider the effect we have on others. If we decided to be more considerate, caring, and less selfish it would really change so much. It would make a difference in the lives around us, slowly we would notice the difference it makes inside our own selves … I wonder if society as a whole would improve if we just switched from the ways we are accustomed to living. In our world everybody just worries about their own needs, wants, wins .. in my opinion these choices leave a dark smudge which smears over time inside of ourselves. As much as our nature is dark it is also very bright, we do make choices to what we will do ,like,want,accept etc and these outward choices effect us inside of our souls…our minds and our whole existence shifts with each decision and whether we like it or not if we constantly choose the dark it does burden us , we are not wired to just be so evil. I think it's sad that very little consideration goes into how will this decision I make effect others, we always tell ourselves it's only our feelings and wants that matter but we do carry the hurt and disregard of others with us, subconsciously it eats away at our inner peace , sometimes we don't even admit the cause for our own disintegration .

****

Labels

I feel so uneasy about labels. In the world we live in everything and everyone has a label. We label our emotions, feelings, behavior, how we present ourselves, our health, our sexuality, our stature etc. Everything in existence ,inside us ,around us has a label. A lot of these labels are limiting and do not capture the fullness of anything instead they box in and restrict . A lot of our labels we then turn and use and react to negatively. I noticed in myself when I label even a feeling it leaves me in a negative state I wonder sometimes if it's the fact that labels confuse me since I don't feel comfortable with them ,they do not capture anything correctly for me -or is it the fact that society has a negative view to basically every label….the funny thing is our opinions on the labels conflict and we focus on the generality of it all and miss the wholeness of the thing labeled.

****

I KEEP ATTEMPTING AT LOVE WITH OTHERS BUT THINGS NEVER GO MY WAY …SO I SEARCH FOR YOU IN MY DREAMS AND REMEMBER US BACK IN THE DAY. MY HEART BREAKS BECAUSE I JUST CAN'T UNDERSTAND…HOW DID YOU EVER MAKE IT WORK WITH ANOTHER …AND I CAN'T FIND YOUR REPLACEMENT IN ANY MAN.

I see a glimmer of hope in him
I do love him very much
The difference between our love and the one he and I share
There are parts of me he hates so much

So I question if I am loved by him
The way that you loved me
He rejects parts of my being
I refuse to not be free

But then I look at what we shared
You did not understand me as well
You accepted blindly
Then left me in a living hell

I guess in my heart there are two loves
How could that ever be
Yet in life I walk alone
No one to care…to share with….or to love me

I guess his love seems a bit more healthy
The one from you was unrealistic and one I cannot do
Somehow I lose strength to try however
What if I am meant to forever be blue

He says he does not believe in love
He complains about things I cannot change
You wanted to share me with another
I alone hurt from my two loves….how strange

******

She sat alone , there was an irreplaceable peace found in her solitude. Forever she kept her bird close, he was a part of her…she felt him inside of her heart, her soul, inside of every fiber of her very being ….yet she was unable to allow herself to believe in him any longer. No more did she dream of an eternity with him , she saw that her burdens were hers to carry. After putting up so much of herself to survive she could not imagine sharing life with another. She had become as a free spirit …no more as a wild animal, craving and yearning love and affection, comfort and security…but her fear of others and the insecurities which formed when it came to another it was to great , forever she awaited the day to heal …for the Lord to mend that which her life had broken …alone , strong, independent….yet so fragile and so unfulfilled.

He was never able to understand her or love her. Life had formed him into someone who could never be hers, he loved her yet was unable to accept her or give of himself that which she so desperately needed. Together they shared a heart , never fulfilling the destiny of becoming one in love….the two soulmates wandered the Earth broken ,bleeding, never whole. Somehow it just was not meant to be , their fate a sad one….each mourned the loss of the other , each tried to mend and heal , to move forward….yet they hurt and never were able to fully recover from the love they lost when they lost one another.

I will wait for you in eternity , my smile will heal your pain, your love will pause the tears ….until then my beloved I will do as I must in life, I will see you in my dreams and surrender to you there where my inhibitions are none. My heart can no longer take disappointement , I fear we both failed I pray you you find comfort in what remains of life…. I will bravely push forward as I look to our day when I will finally have serenity and you my love.

****On Guard***

Never did I feel secure
Never were you able to reassure
In fact you always deny
But my pain your love could cure

I ran to you
I constantly got up my hope
Yet when I needed it least
You would about not wanting me gloat

It's hard for my pride to admit
But I for you burn a bright flame
Yet you deny me any joy
Throw at me hurtful words and blame

I left others to run to your arms
And you kicked me to the side
But I still somehow can't unlove you
I lose all ego and have little pride

I imagine I love another more
My mind wants to scream it's true
Yet my heart refuses to play along
Deep down I know I just want you

I feel so many emotions
In your presence there's this ease
Since I met you I wanted your forever
But you seem so hard to please

Your time you're so reserved with now
I wonder if for me you even have a need
I guess I'll tone down my feelings once again
As I internally explode and slowly bleed

Maybe I look for another love once again
I think I can never have your heart
Maybe this love with you is one sided after all
I guess I figured as much from the very start.

******

Light and dark, sunshine and rain,freedom and constraint,positive and negative… In life there is a balance which somehow intertwines from it we exist and grow, there is cause and effect, action and inaction …. Destiny as well as many random pieces of life which we are a mere visitor in , our memory does not recall our home before we were given this life… magic which is so vast that even our imaginations cannot phantom what awaits after we serve our time in this life -on this planet-in this time.

***

So many half truths in life, so many that we can't possibly even know what information we have in whole… it seems sometimes as if the knowledge we are given it somehow makes us blind. We blindly trust yet I think our ego is what makes us act this way…it's hard to admit you're on a planet ,a part of a society yet you have little say in what actually unfolds. It's also hard to stand

out not accept what half truths are being fed because the judgement that awaits from others is always waiting. Yet that is what keeps us trapped .
****

***

Your love from so many years ago
It still makes me smile
I am lucky to have been loved so passionately
Nobody ever took your place or had your style

As new encounters disappoint
I revisit the times we had
I guess we weren't meant to be
But many times I'm grateful for what we had

Nobody was ever as romantic
Nobody ever took your place in my heart
I did have feelings for a few others
But you were all I really wanted from start

It's tragic that it would have been hurtful
I don't understand how it seemed like a jinx or spell
But I hope you know I loved you more than any other
I would have fought for you even in hell

You deserved a love that I couldn't seem to give you
Memories somehow still come and they sting
Although I never knew real love after ours
It was so big a lifetime another it's size couldn't bring

I regret so much about things
You were and are the biggest man I know
And when others disappoint and hurt me
I inside where you are hidden find you and it comforts me so

Maybe my love problems may be you
You set the bar too high
Nobody ever felt like my other half
Although I gave it my all and really did try

I think we were too young
Possibly it was too much magic for me to accept
And a few poems I write for others
But you are the main character the one I wish to get back

Our story was so crazy
It still sometimes doesn't make sense
But your brown eyes inspired blue
I many times wish we weren't past tense

It's as if only you got me
Only you understood parts of me that no one else can
And try as I might to forget you
In my heart I still carry you as the only man

Destiny is a funny thing
I don't understand why I kept running away
I think the connection was too strong
I hesitant and cynical never managed to stay

Well here goes hurt again
Disappointed in another try I gave at love with another
And my main comfort and reason I don't really care
It is you …your memory more precious than the presence of any other.
*****

Additional books by Marina Dobrosavljevic "M"

Blue Collection:
Blue ISBN 9781438998244
Last of an Emotion ISBN 9781449024642
Just For My Soul ISBN 9781098969806
Just For My Soul (bonus edition) ISBN 9798592687143

Living In The Real ISBN 9781072024842

Princess Malorove and Other Short Stories ISBN 9781544100616

Awaken Your Mind Resuscitate Your Heart ISBN 9798591125578

Save Our Souls ISBN 9798730717985

Journey ISBN 9798774867738

@bluebym